W9-ART-328

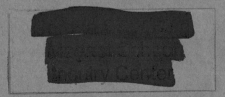

The Little Girl and the Big Bear

For Tanya

Library of Congress Cataloging in Publication Data
Galdone, Joanna.   The little girl and the big bear.
Summary: A retelling of a traditional Slavic tale in which a
clever little girl outwits the bear who is holding her captive
by hiding in a basket of pies.
[1. Folklore, Slavic] I. Galdone, Paul. II. Title.
PZ8.1.G14Li   [398.2] [E]   80-13853
ISBN 0-395-29029-5

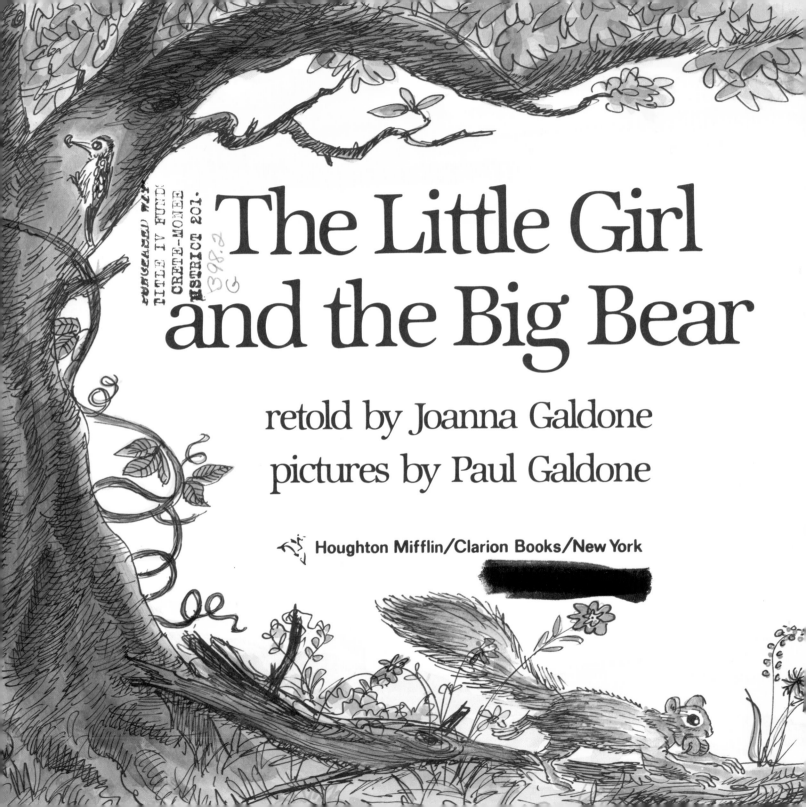

The Little Girl and the Big Bear

retold by Joanna Galdone

pictures by Paul Galdone

Houghton Mifflin/Clarion Books/New York

Once long ago a Little Girl lived
with her grandparents in a village
near a great forest.

One day her friends came by and said,
"The berries in the forest are ripe now.
Let's go and pick them!"

So the Little Girl ran to her grandparents.
"Please let me go to the forest
with my friends," she said.

"Certainly," they said. "But be sure
to stay close to one another."

The Little Girl and her friends ran
deep into the forest.
"Look at all the berries!" they exclaimed.

By and by the Little Girl said,
"My basket is filled to the brim!"
But when she turned around,
there was no one in sight.

"Yoo-hoo! Helloooo!" she called.
"Yoo-hoo! Hellooo!" her call
echoed back to her.
She had wandered far away from her friends.
"I'll have to find my way back alone,"
she thought.

So the Little Girl climbed up hills, and
jumped across streams, and crawled over
boulders. All through the forest she walked,
but she couldn't find her way home.

At last she reached a part of the forest
full of tangled vines, and huge trees
that seemed to stare at her in the dusk.
Then just ahead she saw a little hut.
She knocked on the door, but there was no
answer. So she gave the door a push
and it swung open.

"Who lives here, in the wildest and thickest part of the forest?" the Little Girl wondered as she peered inside. "And why aren't they home?"

It was getting dark.
"I might as well stay here for the night," the Little Girl thought. "Then I'll try to find my way home in the morning."

She had just sat down on a bench to rest when suddenly she heard a great ROAR that made her jump up with a start.

In through the door walked a huge Bear.
He stopped short and growled down at the
Little Girl. But then he smiled and said,

"Oh me, oh my!
What a fine surprise!
I can't believe my very own eyes!
A tempting dinner you'd make, it's true,
But I've a better idea—
Here's what I'll do:

You will be my servant,
Faithful and true.
You'll sweep my floor,
You'll set my table.
You'll take care of me
As long as you're able.
And I'll NEVER let you go!"

The Little Girl cried and cried
for a long time. But it was no use.
She had to stay and keep house
for the Bear just as he had said.

Early every morning the Bear tramped off
into the woods and left the Little Girl alone
for the whole day. But each time before
he left he said,
   "Little Girl, Little Girl,
     Don't run away.
     Here in my hut
     You must stay!"

And the Little Girl did stay,
for she was afraid to disobey him.

But one morning the Little Girl thought,
"Grandma and Grandpa will be so worried
about me. I must try to escape!"
So after the Bear had left for the day
she tiptoed out of the hut and quietly
walked into the forest.

She hadn't gone far when she heard a growl
behind her. The Bear came running and said,

"If you try this again
You know what I'll do?
I'll chop you in pieces
and cook up a stew!"

The Little Girl wanted to get home alive,
so she walked sadly back to the hut.
That night she lay in her cot beside the fire
and thought about how she could get away
from the Bear. All around stretched the great forest.
There was no one to ask which way to go.
Day after day she thought and she thought,
until at last she had an idea.

One evening when the Bear came back from
the forest the Little Girl said to him,
"Please, Bear, let me go home for a day
to see Grandma and Grandpa. I miss them
so much, and want to bring them something
good to eat."

The Bear replied,
    "What you'd do on your own,
        Is simple to tell
        So *I'll* take them the goodies—
        I know the woods well."

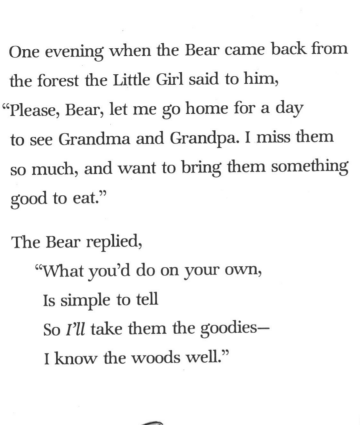

Now that was just what the Little Girl wanted.
Early the next morning she baked some delicious
berry pies and put them on a plate.
Then she got out a large basket.

When the Bear came into the kitchen,
the Little Girl said, "I'll put the pies
in this basket so you can carry them to
Grandma and Grandpa. You must promise not to
stop along the way and eat them. I'm going
to climb to the top of the tallest oak tree, and
from there I'll be able to see everything you do!"

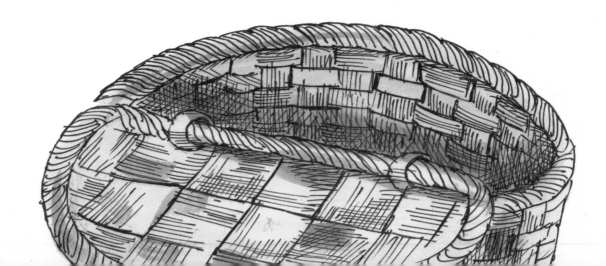

"Give the basket to me,
And I'll do as you say.
I know the way well,
I'll be back in a day,"
said the Bear.

"Do I hear rain on the roof?" asked the Little Girl. "The pies mustn't get wet."

While the Bear went outside to look, the Little Girl quickly got into the basket, put the pies over her head, and closed the lid.

"It's not raining—the sun is shining!"
said the Bear when he came back in.
But the Little Girl was nowhere in sight.

The Bear looked all around the hut for her, and then said,
"She must have climbed into the oak tree already.
Mmmm, those pies smell good. I think I'll
have a look."

He lifted the lid of the basket and peeped
inside. The Little Girl held her breath.
"So many juicy pies!" said the Bear.
But he had promised not to eat them,
so he closed the lid.

"My, those pies are heavy," thought the Bear
as he slung the basket on his back and
started off for the Little Girl's village.

He tramped uphill past the spruce trees.
He clumped downhill around the birch trees.
Stomp-stomp, he clambered over rocks and
boulders. *Kerplash*, he splashed through
streams.

He tramped and stomped and clumped and
splashed till at last he was so tired he
had to stop.

"My feet are so weary,

My back is aching!

Those pies would taste good now,

They're mine for the taking!"

said the Bear as he sat down on a rock to rest.

But the Little Girl called out in a small voice,

as if she were a long way away,

"I see you! I see you!

Get back on your feet!

Get on with your walk,

Not one pie may you eat!"

"Dear me," thought the Bear, "what sharp
eyes that girl has. She sees everything!"

The Bear walked on and on
till he could walk no more.

So he stopped and said again,
   "My feet are so weary,
    My back is aching!
    Those pies would taste good now,
    They're mine for the taking!"

But the Little Girl called out again,
   "I see you! I see you!
    Get back on your feet!
    Get on with your walk,
    Not one pie may you eat!"

So tramp-tramp, clumpity-clump,
stompitty-stomp, and kersplishity-splash,
the Bear went on, a little faster than before.

At last he reached the village, and soon
he found the cottage where the Little Girl's
Grandmother and Grandfather lived.

Knock! Knock!
The Bear banged on the gate
as hard as he could.

"Open the gate!
    I have a surprise.
    Your granddaughter sends you
    A basket of pies!"
he growled.

Soon the village dogs smelled the Bear.
From every yard ran all kinds and sizes
of dogs, just as the Little Girl had thought
they would.
"Ki-yip! Ki-yap! Wawoof! Arraff!" the dogs cried
as they raced toward the Bear.

The Bear's fur bristled. He set down the basket
with a thump and began to run, with all the dogs
following close behind.

At the edge of the forest the Bear stopped.
Quickly the dogs surrounded him. The Bear
growled down at them and they all growled back.

Suddenly a little dog rushed up to the Bear
and nipped at his heels.

The Bear reared up.
With one last great growl he ran off into the forest,
and never once looked back.

The Little Girl's Grandmother and Grandfather heard
all the commotion and hurried to the gate.

"What's in the basket?" the Grandmother asked.
The Grandfather lifted the top.
A face dripping red and·purple
looked up at them.

"Grandma! Grandpa!" the face said, and then
the Little Girl stood up.
The old man and the old woman were overjoyed.
There was their granddaughter, dripping with
berry juice from the broken pies, but
alive and well.

The Grandmother
and Grandfather
didn't mind
the juice.

They kissed and hugged
the Little Girl, and
she kissed and hugged
them back.

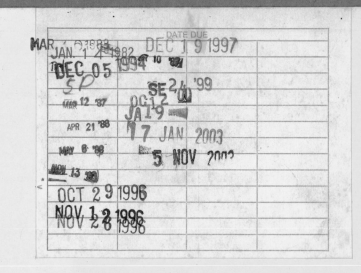
398.2
G

Galdone, Joanna.

The little girl and
the big bear.

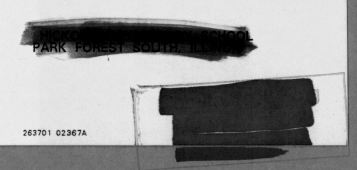